THE MONSTER

Lie

By Lynne Hanson

www.hansonreading.com

CREEKSIDE PUBLISHING

Dedicated to that still small voice within each of us
that helps us to be honest. - Lynne Hanson

The Monster Lie

by Lynne Hanson

Published by Creekside Publishing
All rights reserved. No part of this publication may be used or reproduced in
any manner whatsoever without the written permission of Lynne Hanson.
For information regarding permission, write to Creekside Publishing,
2310 Homestead Rd. Suite C-1, 155, Los Altos, CA 94024-7302.
First published in the United States by Creekside Publishing in 2016
Illustrated by Erik Lobo
Design by Amanda Allen

ISBN-13: 978-0692697504
ISBN-10: 0692697500

For information visit www.hansonreading.com

CREEK SIDE
PUBLISHING

I was in Mrs. Bixby's class. It had been such a good year, but it didn't end well. On the last day of school before summer vacation, I told a lie.

I didn't think it was a big lie, but I knew it was wrong. What I didn't know was how lies grow.

1

It all started when Mrs. Bixby went around the room asking each kid what they were going to do for summer vacation.

My classmates' summer plans seemed
so exciting! Nate was even going to
Mount Rushmore!

Jill and her dad were going to a huge amusement park.

Bo, the best artist in the class, won a vacation at a special art camp for children.

Jason, who was mega-brainy, was going to build a robot.

We couldn't afford to take a big vacation. Dad was saving up for a better car, which we really needed.

I felt like the only kid in school who didn't have any plans to talk about.

Mrs. Bixby stopped at my desk and said, "Tell us what you are going to be doing over the summer, Willis."

Before I knew it, a little lie just snuck out of my mouth. "We're going to Amsterdam," I said.

I guess Amsterdam came to mind because my grandmother had been born there. She loved to read me stories about Holland, which is part of the Netherlands.

The whole class focused on me, and then I wished I hadn't said anything. I hoped Mrs. Bixby would just move on to the next kid, but she just stood there, waiting.

When I didn't say anything, Mrs. Bixby smiled, "Wow! That sounds like a wonderful adventure. I hope you have a great time. Who are you going with?"

"I'm going with my grandparents," I said.

I felt so bad. I wanted to make my mouth stop talking, but the lie kept getting bigger and bigger.

She said, "Will you visit the famous Van Gogh Museum in Amsterdam?"
(pronounced: Van-GO)

I had no idea about any *Van Gogh Museum*. Boy, was I glad when she finally stopped asking me questions and moved on!

I thought that would be the end of it.

School let out, and I probably wouldn't see Mrs. Bixby again.

Summer began, and
even though we didn't
go anywhere, I still
had lots of fun.

17

My grandparents visited every Sunday and played board games with us. They always brought awesome desserts too!

Most of my days were spent outside skateboarding around the neighborhood.

I read comic books, drank orange soda and ginger ale, and completely forgot about Amsterdam.

All too soon school was starting.
I was beginning a new grade. To my
surprise, I had the same teacher,
Mrs. Bixby.

Mrs. Bixby greeted me at the door, "Great to see you again, Willis."

23

The day started great. During the first recess, I got to play with some of my friends from the year before.

We took our seats, and Mrs. Bixby wrote in giant letters on the board, "What I Did on My Summer Vacation."

You might have thought I'd lose my marbles right then. But when you lie, you don't remember what you said. I didn't think much of it. Writing about your summer vacation is the same assignment teachers always make you do.

Then the worst thing happened! Mrs. Bixby asked me to come up in front of the class.

"I'm so excited to hear about your trip to Amsterdam!" she said.

Oh, my gosh! I had forgotten all about Amsterdam. That lie was coming back to haunt me, and it was bigger than ever. I felt sick.

There I was standing in front of the whole class. I just stood there, wishing I could dig a deep hole under the teacher's desk and crawl into it.

Before I could really think, Mrs. Bixby said, "Come on. Everyone is waiting."

The teacher kept asking me questions, and I kept making up answers. I didn't want the lie to grow anymore, but I wasn't smart enough to get out of it.

The lie was like a monster getting
bigger and bigger and was crushing
me. I felt so awful.

Mrs. Bixby was amazed. She kept smiling and asking more questions, and I kept feeling sicker and sicker. My friends were staring at me wide-eyed, hanging on my every word. Then, finally, it was over!

Later, at recess all the kids wanted to play with me. I was the first one chosen for kickball!

Jill made a crown for me out of
construction paper that said "Prince
of the Netherlands." All of a sudden,
I was so popular.

I was treated like a hero for the rest of the day, but I felt like a liar and a cheat!

Somehow, you don't remember lies very long. Being popular doesn't last very long either.

Everything settled back to normal. Even that sick feeling went away, until the day Mom volunteered at school.

When I came home she said, "Willis, how was your trip to Holland?"

Oh no! My lie popped like a fat
balloon. The monster lie was
loose for all to see.

Mom had always told me that it was very important to be honest so I could be trusted. She wrapped her arm around me.

"Willis, being popular or having something interesting to say is not as important as being trustworthy. If you are honest in what you say and do, everyone will learn to trust you. The reputation you build can open or close doors for you depending on the choices you make."

Dad was disappointed in me. We had a talk about the importance of being honest.

Dad told me that it took a long time to build a good reputation and only a few hasty mistakes to destroy it.

It was an awful weekend.

I knew my teacher thought I was a liar, all the parent volunteers thought I was a liar, and my friends would find out too. I felt so terrible and so ashamed. My reputation was ruined!

When Monday came, I dreaded going back to school and facing everyone. I would have pretended to be sick, but my mom knew better. I had no appetite and couldn't even eat my breakfast.

I put on my backpack and dragged myself to school.

On the way to class I bumped into Mrs. Bixby.

"I'm sorry I lied about my vacation," I said. I hoped an apology would make me feel better.

To my surprise, Mrs. Bixby smiled, "I'm so glad you were brave enough to apologize," she told me.

"I told everyone that my dad was an international super spy for the CIA. Of course, the story caused a big mess, and I ended up looking so foolish.

Willis, most children lie sometime. It's just a part of growing-up. It is so easy to let a little exaggeration or a little lie get bigger and bigger."

52

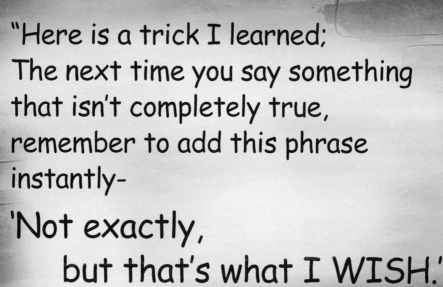

"Here is a trick I learned;
The next time you say something
that isn't completely true,
remember to add this phrase
instantly-

'Not exactly,
          but that's what I WISH.'

You must say
it instantly,
or the lie will
trap you."

53

"OK, I will!" I said. I hugged Mrs. Bixby and I never forgot what she said.

Now, I am an adult and that phrase has stopped a lot of little lies from getting me into big trouble.

I always tell this story to my class at the beginning of each school year before I ask them what they did on their summer vacation.

"Any questions?"

"How do we know this story is true?"

I am glad I have a mom and dad who thought it was important to tell the truth and a teacher who helped me learn how. I hope my story will help you too!

Now, what did you do on your summer vacation?"

Read more Willis stories in the
HANSON Reading Phonics Chart System Books.

Made in the USA
Columbia, SC
04 September 2017